TIKVAH
MEANS HOPE

P9-DMC-574

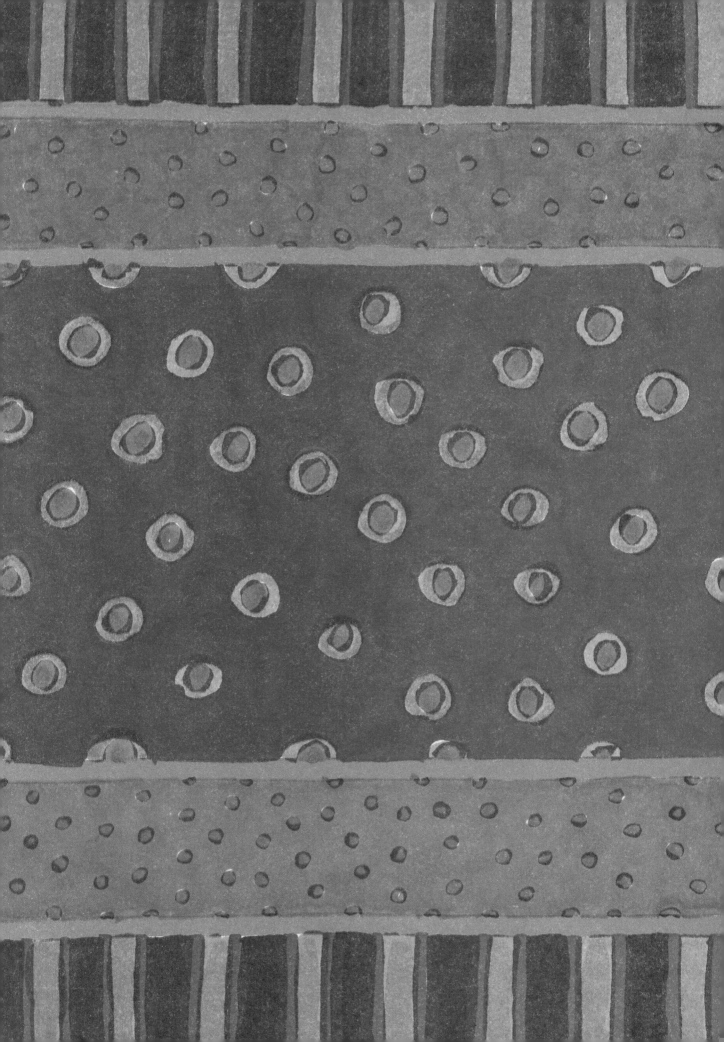

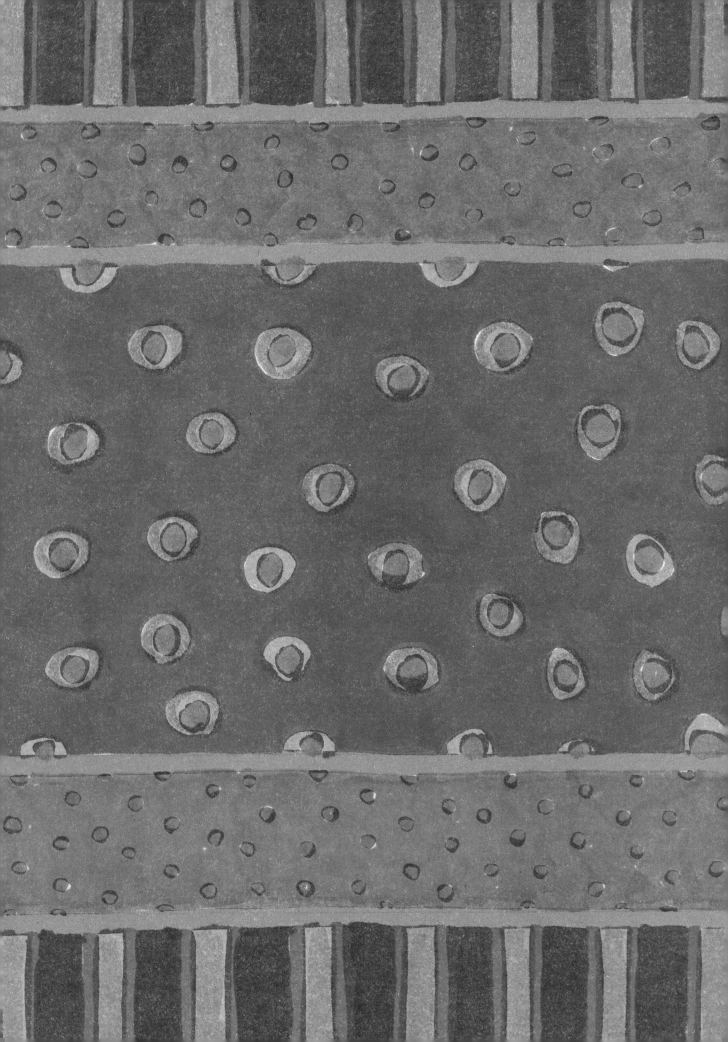

Patricia Polacco

TIKVAH
MEANS HOPE

A Picture Yearling Book

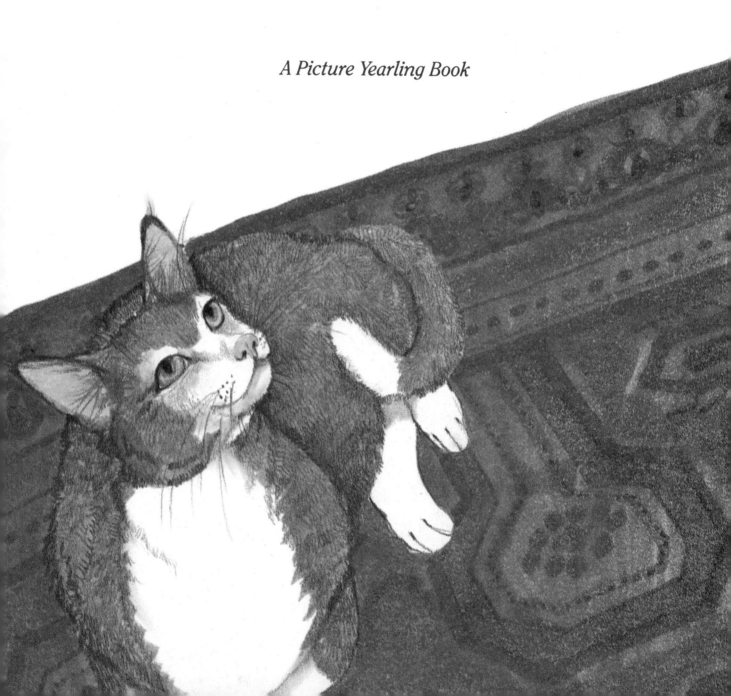

Published by
Bantam Doubleday Dell Books for Young Readers
a division of
Bantam Doubleday Dell Publishing Group, Inc.
1540 Broadway
New York, New York 10036

If you purchased this book without a cover you should be aware that this book is
stolen property. It was reported as "unsold and destroyed" to the publisher and
neither the author nor the publisher has received any payment for this
"stripped book."

Copyright © 1994 by Patricia Polacco

All rights reserved. No part of this book may be reproduced or transmitted in any form
or by any means, electronic or mechanical, including photocopying, recording, or by any
information storage and retrieval system, without the written permission of the
Publisher, except where permitted by law. For information address Doubleday Books
for Young Readers, New York, New York 10036.

The trademarks Yearling® and Dell® are registered in the U.S. Patent and Trademark
Office and in other countries.

ISBN: 0-440-41229-3

Reprinted by arrangement with Doubleday Books for Young Readers

Printed in the United States of America

September 1996

10 9 8 7 6 5 4 3 2 1

DAN

In loving memory of Herman and Hannah Roth

To the amazing people of Oakland,
and
To fire fighters everywhere,
Thank you

Tikvah watched the jay as it fluttered onto the railing. It was a bright October morning, dry and warm. Mr. Roth stood deep in thought, gazing out at his back yard. Justine, his next-door neighbor, watched his face. She knew an important decision was at hand.

"Yes, I think that's exactly where we shall build it this year!" Mr. Roth finally announced.

"We have our thanksgiving dinners inside our house," Justine said as they walked down to the lower yard.

"I know," Mr. Roth answered. "But we have our thanksgiving in the Sukkah. You see, we Jews have always had to move a lot. We wandered in the desert for many, many years. Then, at long last we found the Promised Land and settled into real homes. Now we build these little huts to remind us of all the days that we had no place to live, and also to give thanks for our new homes and the rich harvest that our new land gave us."

"Are you gonna build it here?" Duane called out as he ran up the path. He lived down the street and he was Justine's best friend.

Mr. Roth smiled at him. "I'm so glad you're here to help, Duane. Maybe you can hand me those palm branches?"

They all helped tie pieces of cloth onto the sides. Then Justine and Duane tied fruit and gourds from the palms.

"Listen to those birds sing." Mr. Roth sighed happily. "I think this is going to be the best Sukkoth ever!"

Mrs. Roth came to join them. "Lemon cake and hot chocolate for the workers," she announced. Then she stood, admiring the Sukkah.

"Isn't it perfect," she said. "Every year your Sukkahs get more beautiful! I'm sure because you have such help." And she pinched Justine's chin.

"I can't wait for tonight," Duane whispered as he gave Justine their secret handshake.

When evening finally came, Justine was so excited about spending the night in the Sukkah that she almost forgot to pack her special pillow, the one with no feathers because of her asthma. She kissed the photo of her grandma in New Jersey and ran for the front door.

"Hey, where's my sugar?" her mother asked. Justine gave her folks the biggest hugs and butterfly kisses.

"Don't let the bedbugs bite, and sleep tight," her dad called as Justine hurried out the front door.

Duane folded his pajamas into a bundle and stuffed them into his duffel bag.

"I'm amazed you could even find your jammies in this mess," his mother said.

"Mom, I'm not a baby. I don't wear jammies!"

His father stuck his head in the door. "Oh, so you're all grown up, are you? Well then, guess you don't have to worry about any bears while you sleep under the stars, huh?" he joked.

"Dad! There aren't any bears in the Oakland hills!" Duane protested. "Don't touch my baseball cards," he warned his little brother Barry.

"Don't let Barry mess with any of my stuff," Duane hollered as he ran by his little brother and out the front door.

Duane and Justine settled into the Sukkah while the crickets chirped a nighttime chorus. They watched the lights from the houses in the hills behind them flicker like stars. When Mr. Roth came in, he stood quietly for a moment. They all listened as an owl made a soft hooting sound.

"Such glory," Mr. Roth finally said. "To lie here and look up through the palm branches at the stars. We have always built our Sukkahs this way, so we can see the sky at night."

Tikvah burrowed her way under Justine's blanket, then started to purr.

"So it's here you're going to stay tonight, is it?" Mr. Roth said, patting her. "Now get some sleep. Tomorrow is going to be a busy day." He blew them all a kiss before he left.

The next morning it was very hot.

"Too hot for October," Mr. Roth said. He was driving to the market with Justine and Duane. "Now let me see. To make our feast in the Sukkah the best ever, we have to get ground beef from the butcher, then cabbage from the greengrocer for my Hannah's cabbage rolls. Such cabbage rolls she makes!"

A strong gust of hot wind blew his hat down the street when they walked toward Enzo's butcher shop.

"Strange day, isn't it?" Enzo said.

Mr. Wilson came running into the shop. "Did you hear?" he asked, breathing hard. "There's a terrible fire in the hills!"

They all ran outside to see where he was pointing.

"That's where I live!" a woman screamed.

Duane and Justine started to feel uneasy as more and more people collected on the sidewalk to watch.

"The sun is an orange ball," Justine cried. "We can look right at it!"

"What is all this stuff?" Duane asked. He caught what looked like a black leaf that floated down from the sky.

"There's writing on it," Enzo said, looking closely at it. "It's in Italian. It's a page from a cookbook!"

"Someone's kitchen is on fire," Mr. Roth said quietly.

More and more black leaves fell on them, and the sky started to darken. There was smoke everywhere. Sirens were sounding all over the city. Cars were zooming down the street. People were running, and everyone looked scared.

"I want my momma." Justine started to cry.

"Please, Mr. Roth," Duane said, "let's go home!"

They got into the car and drove toward home, but a fire fighter stopped them halfway up their hill. "But we live up there!" Mr. Roth argued.

"All of the families from this neighborhood are being evacuated. Some of them are over there," the fire fighter said as he motioned toward a crowd. "The rest are at Oakland Tech, in the gym."

Justine spotted her mother and father in the crowd. "Momma," she cried as she ran to them.

Duane's family was standing next to Mrs. Roth. She was crying. "We had no time to get anything! I couldn't find Tikvah. I called and called, but she didn't come. Our poor little *kattileh*."

Mr. Roth spoke softly to her. "It could have been worse. All of our friends and their precious children are right here with us."

Then he gently rocked her in his arms.

They all just stood and watched in horror until the fire fighters asked them to move to the gym for their own safety. They spent the night there while Oakland burned.

The fire burned for two days. More and more people came to the gym looking for family, or for a place to stay, or just to get a warm meal and much-needed sleep. Everyone got clothes from boxes that other people brought.

When it was all over, everyone went home to their neighborhood together. They didn't even recognize their own street. Everything was gone, even the street signs. Only the chimneys still stood, marking the places where their homes had been.

The birds, squirrels, raccoons, and deer were all gone. There were no photographs of grandmothers from New Jersey, no favorite baseball cards, and no Tikvah!

The Roths called and called for Tikvah as they sifted through piles of rubble and ashes.

Mr. Roth started crying. "If only I could find something, anything, that would prove I had a life here."

Duane and Justine were breathless and smiling as they ran up to him.

"Come quick, you have to see!" they called excitedly.

Mr. and Mrs. Roth followed them down into what used to be the yard.

They couldn't believe what they saw there. "The wind must have changed," Mrs. Roth murmured.

"No," Mr. Roth said through his tears, "it's a miracle."

The Sukkah had not burned.

Not a leaf of the palm branches, not a piece of cloth, not even the vegetables or fruit!

The stars were especially bright that night. All the neighbors gathered together. Everyone brought food.

The candles on the table flickered as Mr. Roth prayed.

"We should be very thankful that we have good food, friends, and our lives," he said quietly.

But no one seemed happy at all. Everything was so still. No sounds of crickets or owls or barking dogs—only deafening silence.

Just then, a tiny squeak came from somewhere near the barbecue pit.

Mr. Roth reached under the barbecue.

"There's something here!" he said, surprised. He reached farther in. "It's something furry and warm."

"Be careful, dear," Mrs. Roth warned.

"It's moving into my hands—now it's licking! That kiss I'd know anywhere!"

Mr. Roth lifted Tikvah out of the darkness. She was a little singed, and very hungry—but she was alive!

Then the celebration rang out!

Through the darkness of the blackened hills, there was singing, there was remembering and crying, and lots of hugging and laughter, too.

Justine and Duane needed to hold that little cat, but when they finally gave her back to Mr. Roth, he held her close, next to his heart.

"Do you know what her name means in Hebrew?" he said, wiping away his tears. "It means hope!"

AUTHOR'S NOTE:

It has been over two years since the firestorm here in Oakland. It has been called the worst disaster of its kind in the history of our country. Over three thousand four hundred houses were burned to the ground. All the families that lived in them were made homeless in a matter of hours. The sense of loss is so far-reaching that no emotional words can describe it. Twenty-five people lost their lives, one of them a fire fighter.

Besides the toll in human terms, the impact of the loss of the wildlife as well as family pets is still felt. Most pets that were in their homes that hot Sunday morning perished. The ones that did survive now wander the hills and have reverted to the wild. Acres of trees and vegetation have virtually disappeared from the Bay Area, and some species will never grow there again.

Some of the thousands who lost their homes have rebuilt. Some could not bear to return to what was, and always will be, a painful reminder of their tragic loss. Some have moved to other parts of the country.

For those of us who remain here in Oakland, a sense of community has welded our spirits together. We still share our lives, our memories, and most of all, hope!

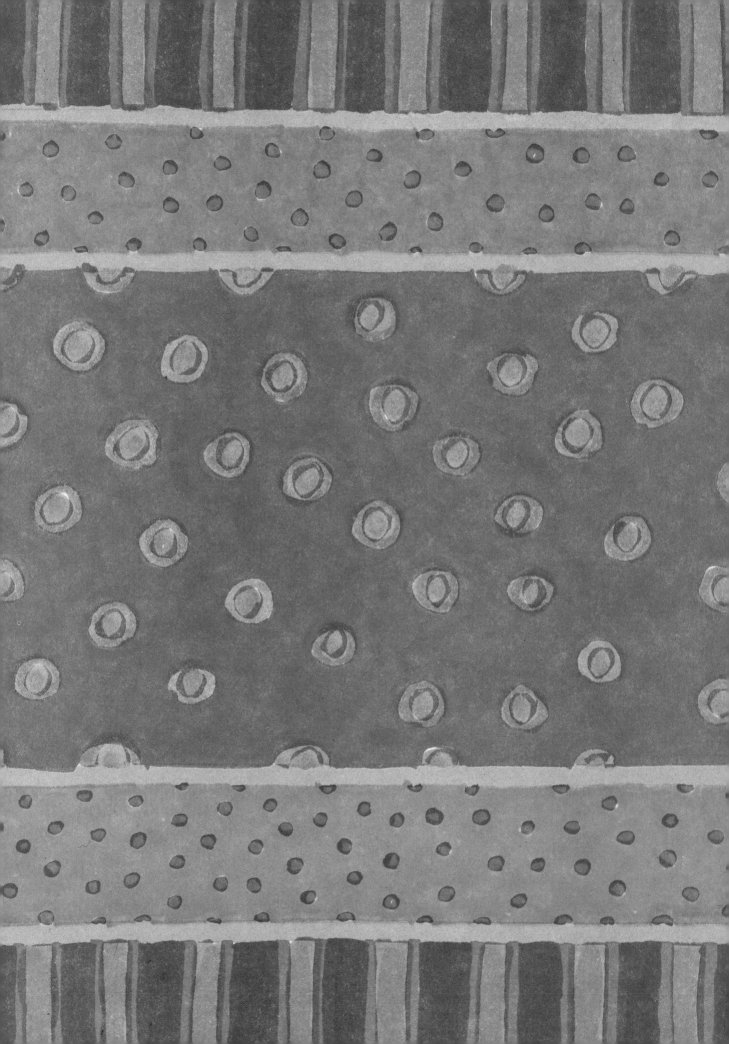

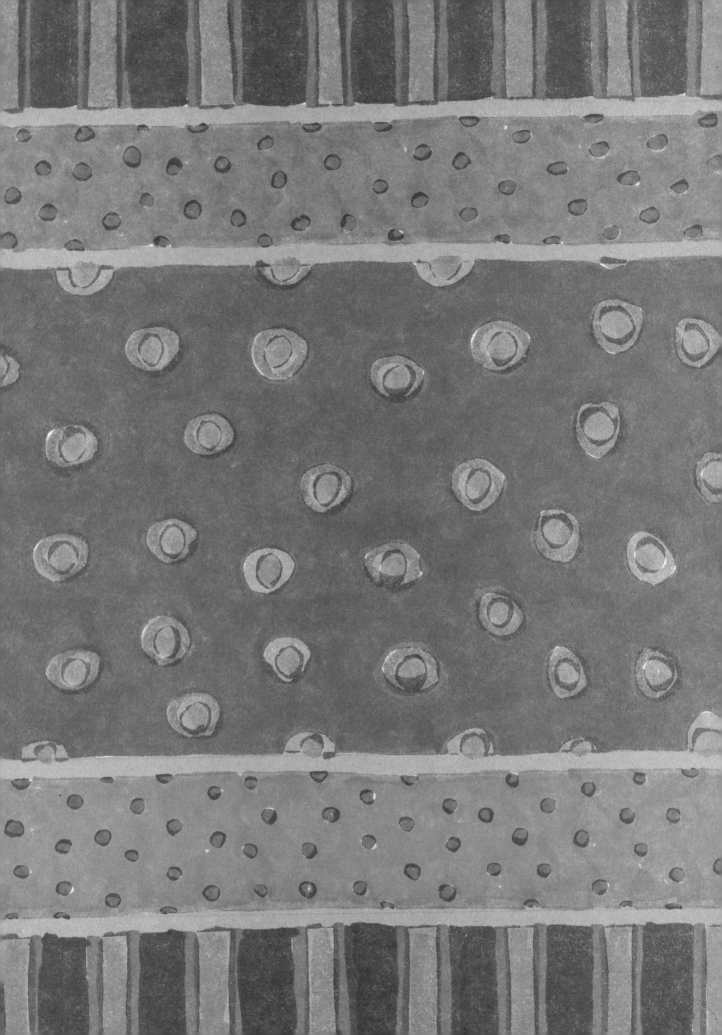